A BEACON ✦ BIOGRAPHY

MALALA

Kayleen Reusser

YOUSAFZAI

PURPLE TOAD
PUBLISHING

PURPLE TOAD
PUBLISHING

Printing   1   2   3   4   5   6   7   8   9

A Beacon Biography

Angelina Jolie
Big Time Rush
Carly Rae Jepsen
Drake
Ed Sheeran
Harry Styles of One Direction
Jennifer Lawrence
Kevin Durant
Lorde
Malala
Markus "Notch" Persson, Creator of Minecraft
Mo'ne Davis
Muhammad Ali
Neil deGrasse Tyson
Peyton Manning
Robert Griffin III (RG3)

Publisher's Cataloging-in-Publication Data
Reusser, Kayleen.
 Malala / written by Kayleen Reusser.
  p. cm.
     Includes bibliographic references and index.
     ISBN 9781624691836
1. Yousafzai, Malala, 1997—Juvenile literature. 2. Women social reformers—Pakistan--Biography—Juvenile literature. I. Series: Beacon Biographies Collection Two.
 LC2330 2016
 371.822095491
                                        Library of Congress Control Number: 2015941407

eBook ISBN: 9781624691843

ABOUT THE AUTHOR: Kayleen Reusser is author of a dozen children's books. She lives in Indiana and travels all over the country speaking to children and other groups about the craft of writing. Find out more at http://www.KayleenR.com.

PUBLISHER'S NOTE: The data in this book has been researched in depth, and to the best of our knowledge is factual. Although every measure is taken to give an accurate account, Purple Toad Publishing makes no warranty of the accuracy of the information and is not liable for damages caused by inaccuracies. This story has not been authorized or endorsed by Malala Yousafzai.

CONTENTS

Malala Yousafzai

*Sir de pa lowara tega kegda
Praday watan de paki nishta
balakhtona*

O Wayfarer! Rest your head on
the stony cobblestone
It is a foreign land—not the
city of your kings!

Nightmare

Malala Yousafzai slowly opened her eyes. Her lids felt heavy. The fifteen-year-old was tempted to drift back to sleep on the soft bed, but she forced herself to look around.

What she saw terrified her. Nothing looked familiar. Instead of clothes strewn about her bedroom in Mingora, Pakistan, she saw white walls. Strangers wearing some type of uniforms—medical?— moved about. They spoke with British accents. Malala had studied the English language at her school in Swat Valley, so she understood them.

She sensed they were doctors and nurses and she was in a hospital. Where was her family?

Panic rose in Malala's throat. She didn't remember anything. How long had she lain there?[1]

Her shoulder throbbed and the left side of her face ached. Lifting a hand, Malala felt her head. It was swathed in bandages. What had happened to her?

She opened her mouth to ask questions but no sound came out. A man who she thought might be a doctor hurried to her side. He explained she was a patient at Queen Elizabeth Hospital in Birmingham, England. A breathing tube in her neck prevented her from speaking.

Medical staff at Queen Elizabeth's Hospital cared for Malala after she was shot.

Malala's mind raced. Why was she in England? No one in her family—father, Ziauddin; mother, Tor Pekai; and brothers, 13-year-old Khushal and 8-year-old Atal—had ever left Pakistan. One needed a passport to leave the country, and they didn't own passports.

When she thought of her family, her heart filled with fear. She knew they loved her and would never leave her. Were they alive?[2]

Malala's hospital room had no windows, but she could hear muted sounds of traffic. Thankfully, one thing she didn't hear was gunfire.

Malala had been born on July 12, 1997, at her family's home in Swat Valley in northwestern Pakistan. It was a beautiful place with snowcapped mountains and green fields.

Her father had founded Khushal School for Girls and was its principal. Malala attended the school, while her two younger brothers were enrolled in another one. (In Pakistan, girls and boys attend separate schools.) Malala's mother cared for the family at home. Malala loved her home. In summer, birds devoured fruit from a plum tree in the family's front yard. Grapes, guavas, and persimmons grew in their garden.

All her life Malala had heard about the conflicts in Pakistan. Ever since the country was created in 1947, wars had taken place there and many leaders had attempted to rule. Malala's favorite, Benazir Bhutto, served as Pakistan's first female prime minister from 1988 to 1990. She served a second term from 1993 to 1996. "She symbolized the end of dictatorship and the beginning of democracy," Malala wrote in her book, *I Am Malala*.[3]

Benazir Bhutto served as Pakistan's first female prime minister.

Pakistan was created in 1947 as an independent Muslim nation.

Bhutto left the country in exile in 1999 but returned in 2007. A few months later, she was assassinated.

The unstable Pakistani government made it easy for enemies to take control. When Malala was ten years old, a terrorist group called the Taliban invaded. Seeing them on the streets of Mingora, carrying guns with long, straggly hair and beards and stockings over their heads terrified her.

Only one thing was scarier than the Taliban's appearance—their abuse of power. They forced Pakistani people to run businesses and schools by their own strict laws. They burned people's TVs, DVDs and CDs and prohibited dancing, stating it was sinful to listen to certain types of music. They closed beauty parlors and banned barbers and shopping malls. They didn't even allow polio vaccinations. If a person disobeyed, Taliban soldiers would whip them in public.

The Pakistani government tried to fight the Taliban. Malala and her family were often woken at night by the boom of cannon and the chatter of machine guns.[4]

Malala's home, Swat Valley, was a beautiful place with snowcapped mountains and green fields.

Students whose schools were bombed by the Taliban were forced to hold classes outside.

In 2007, the Taliban began bombing Pakistani schools. By the end of 2008, they had destroyed 400.[5]

To make matters worse, in December 2008 the terrorists announced all-girls schools in Pakistan would close the following month. Eleven-year-old Malala wondered how they could stop 50,000 girls from attending school in the twenty-first century.[6]

When it seemed no one would try to stop the Taliban, Malala was devastated. She nearly gave in to hopelessness. She said, "I thought I would never be able to become a doctor. I would never be able to be who I wanted to be . . . my life would be just getting married at the age of 13 or 14."[7]

Instead, she decided to fight back.

Malala's family supported her decision to remain in school despite fear of the Taliban.

Living Among the Taliban

Malala's father not only taught her math and physics, but he also showed her how to pay attention to governmental problems. Malala and Ziauddin Yousafzai encouraged people in Swat Valley not to be intimidated by the Taliban.[1]

When some of her classmates withdrew from school, Malala understood their fear. Yet, she was thankful for the support she received from her parents. "They never once suggested I should withdraw from school," she wrote. "Though we loved school, we hadn't realized how important education was until the Taliban tried to stop us. Going to school, reading and doing our homework wasn't just a way of passing time. It was our future."[2]

Focusing on schoolwork had been a way for Malala to keep from thinking about the Taliban. "Our school was a haven from the horrors outside," she wrote.[3] When her school closed, she had nothing to distract her from the conflict.

A news reporter for the British Broadcasting Company (BBC) asked Malala to write a blog (online diary) about life growing up as a young girl under Taliban rule. She agreed but used a secret name to keep her identity confidential. Her pen name was Gul Makai (Cornflower), the name of a female character in a Pakistani folk tale.

Malala and the reporter talked on the phone for thirty minutes each week about life in Swat Valley. She also wrote about how difficult it was to be told what music she could listen to, what clothing to wear, and even what colors she could wear (her favorite color is pink).[4] Most of all, Malala talked about the right girls had to education.

During one interview, Malala confessed, "I pictured a Taliban coming with a gun and he wants to shoot me. I thought I would take my shoe and hit him. But if I hit him with a shoe and am cruel to him, it means there is no difference between us." In the Middle East, throwing a shoe at someone is a serious insult. "I want to have peace for their family as well . . . I want to tell Taliban, be peaceful."[5]

Malala was encouraged by the story of Anne Frank, a 13-year-old Jewish girl who hid with her family from the Nazis in Holland during World War II. Anne had also kept a diary about her experiences. Sadly, her family was found. Anne died in a concentration camp at the age of 15. Since being published, *The Diary of Anne Frank* has become a powerful record of forgiveness and strength under pressure.

During World War II, Anne Frank, like Malala, endured persecution because of her religious beliefs.

Malala hoped her words could encourage people to take action for children's education. In a documentary made about her life at this time, Malala said, "They cannot stop me. I will get my education if it's at home, school or somewhere else. This is our request to the world—save our schools, save our Pakistan."[6]

Malala's words appeared weekly on the BBC Urdu web site. People around the world who read it learned about the challenges she and other students endured under the Taliban's abusive power.[7]

As Muslims, Malala and her family often prayed to God for answers to problems. It seemed their prayers had been answered a month later when the Taliban changed its mind—slightly. Instead

Trying to forget the danger, these girls are hard at work studying.

of forbidding all girls from attending school, they decided that girls age 10 and younger could attend classes.

Malala, who only stood five feet, two inches tall, had often prayed God would make her taller. Now she was thankful for her petite size as she and other girls her age pretended to be age 10, hiding books under their shawls while walking to school.[8]

Life in Swat Valley continued to deteriorate. In May 2009, the U.S. government sent troops to help the Pakistani government fight the Taliban. Residents of Swat were advised to leave the area as fighting was expected to be fierce.

Malala's family left their home, wondering if they would ever see it again. For three months, they lived with friends and relatives outside of Swat Valley.

Despite the danger, Malala continued to talk against the Taliban. The more interviews she gave, the stronger she felt. "In my heart was the belief that God would protect me," she wrote. "I am speaking for my rights and the rights of other girls. I am not doing anything wrong. It's my duty. God wants to see how we behave in such situations."[9]

The opportunity to test Malala's faith would arrive sooner than she thought.

Malala and her family often prayed to God for answers to problems with the Taliban.

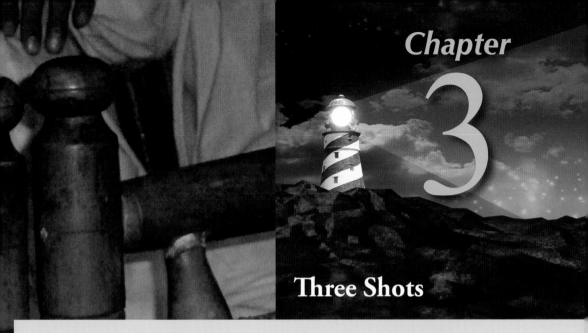

By August 1, 2009, Pakistani military forces had defeated the Taliban. Malala's family joyously returned to their homeland. The ban against girls attending school was lifted and Malala returned to school, eager to talk with friends who had also been Internally Displaced Persons (IDPs).

After being prohibited from attending school, Malala grew more determined than ever to fight for children's rights to education. She provided interviews with news correspondents who traveled to Pakistan to report about the current situation.

"Education is the basic right of every person, including Muslims," she said. "Islam says every girl and boy should go to school. In the Koran it is written, God wants us to have knowledge. He wants us to know why the sky is blue and about oceans and stars."[1] She spoke so well about her home and life that one journalist called her *takra jenai*—'bright shining young lady.'[2]

When the Taliban posted a threat against Malala on the Internet, she did not take it seriously. Her father tried to talk her out of speaking against the terrorists. "You said if we believe in something greater than our lives, our voices will only multiply if we are dead," she told him.[3] She also believed her father's life was more

Malalai lost her life leading Afghan troops into battle.

in danger from terrorists than her own.[4]

Ziauddin couldn't blame his daughter for being brave. After all, he had named her after a heroine who lost her life in battle. In 1880, Malalai, the daughter of a shepherd in Afghanistan, led the Afghan troops in an important victory over the British during the Battle of Maiwand. Malalai died in the battle, making her a kind of martyr.

Malala's father was proud of her courage and her ability to speak about important issues. He was especially nervous, however, in December 2011 when the Pakistani government gave Malala a special award—the country's first National Peace Prize. It was later renamed the Malala Prize and would be awarded annually to activists under 18 years old.

In Pakistani culture, only the dead are honored. Ziauddin worried because he thought Malala's award was a bad omen.[5]

Malala stayed calm and did not admit it to her family, but she was secretly terrified by the Taliban's threats. Each night she checked the locks on the doors and windows of her home. Her sleep was filled with nightmares.

Lying on her hospital bed, thinking about home and her family, Malala felt happy, but as she recalled the fear and danger, new images began to surface. She had been riding a school bus with girlfriends. They talked and laughed as they gossiped and compared their schoolwork.

Then the picture changed. Malala was lying on a stretcher, head bleeding. Two other girls on the bus also had blood on them. The pictures were so vivid and frightening that Malala told herself they were part of a nightmare.

Suddenly she understood. The visions were not a nightmare. Her fear of dying, which she had kept quiet from her parents, had become real. Malala had been shot in the head by a terrorist.

After her stunning realization, Malala wrote questions to the hospital staff, asking to know details of what had happened to her.

They told her that a week earlier, on October 9, 2012, she had been riding the school's bus—a white Toyota truck—to her home after classes at Khushal School. The school was only a five-minute walk from Malala's home, but after threats from the Taliban against Malala's life, her mother insisted that she ride the bus to and from school.

When the bus stopped in the middle of the road, the girls stopped chattering. A gunman appeared at the back of the bus. The girls stared. Despite his rugged appearance, Malala thought he was young, maybe twenty years old. He pointed the gun at the girls. "Who is Malala?" he demanded.

The girls, stunned, sat without replying.

A cultural tradition of the Pakistani people is for females, once they reach puberty, to cover their bodies and faces with a burqa

when they are in public. That day Malala had chosen not to cover her face while riding in the truck.

As Malala was the only girl with her face uncovered, the terrorist believed she was the girl he wanted. Raising his Colt .45, he pointed it at her and pulled the trigger.

Malala sat in the back of this bus.

After being shot, Malala was flown to England and admitted to Queen Elizabeth Hospital.

The gunman fired three shots. The first went through Malala's left eye socket. It punctured her left eardrum before landing in her shoulder. Somehow, the bullet, fired from a few feet away, missed her brain.

The second bullet struck another girl in the truck, Shazia Ramzan, injuring her hand and shoulder. A third bullet traveled through Shazia's shoulder and into the upper right arm of a third girl, Kainat Riaz.

The bus driver rushed the truck to Swat Central Hospital in Mingora, where doctors and nurses treated all three girls.

Although it appeared that Malala was not seriously wounded, her physical condition worsened as hours passed. When her head swelled and her kidneys and liver began to shut down, her parents believed Malala was close to death. They urged people around the world to pray for her.

Medical officials advised Ziauddin and Tor to take Malala to another country for the care she needed. But where?

Doctors Fiona Reynolds and Javid Kayani from England were attending a conference in Pakistan when Malala was attacked. They had often treated British soldiers wounded from wars in Afghanistan and Iraq at Queen Elizabeth Hospital in Birmingham, England. When they heard about Malala's condition, they volunteered to take her to their hospital.

As news about the attack on Malala and the other girls spread around the world, offers of help arrived. Officials of the United Arab Emirates, a country in the Middle East, owned a plane outfitted like an operating room. They volunteered to fly Malala and the doctors to England. Reluctantly, Malala's parents signed forms, allowing her to leave Pakistan without them. They planned to join her as soon as their passports were processed.

Unconscious, Malala was not aware of her trip in the 'flying hospital.' After she had awakened, the doctor informed her that she was in England and that her family was safe and would arrive soon.

Ten days after the shooting, Malala's family arrived in England. With her parents and brothers at her bedside, Malala felt loved and comforted.[1]

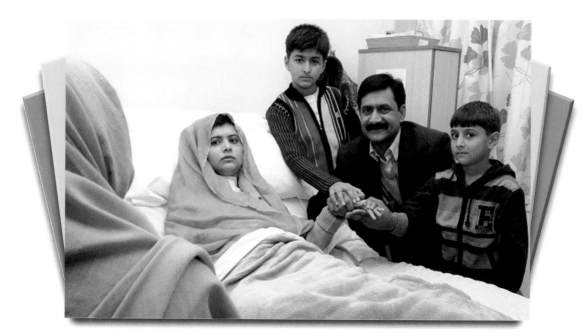

Malala's family had to wait for passports before going to England to be with her.

Malala received thousands of cards from people around the world who were outraged at the attempt on her life and thankful she was alive. Malala and her family believed God had saved her life. "I believe when people pray for life, God gives life," she said. "God listens to his people's voices."[2]

Malala's attack attracted attention from people around the world.

Malala endured many surgeries and hours of therapy to repair the damage to her face, eardrum, and shoulder. In February 2013, she had surgery to fit a titanium plate in her head. She also received a cochlear implant to help her hear in her left ear. She couldn't blink fully. But by April 2013, she was well enough to enroll in school in England.

Malala and her family stayed in England. Her brothers were enrolled in school. Her body will never be exactly the same as it was before the shooting, but Malala tries to maintain a normal lifestyle. She talks online with friends from Pakistan and dreams of the day when she can return to her homeland. Meanwhile, the identity of her assassin is still being investigated.

By this time, Malala had changed her mind about a career. After all the turmoil in her life and the lives of others, she wanted to do more to help. "I want to be a politician," she told one reporter. "I want to be the prime minister of Pakistan."[3]

As for the two other students who were shot in the bus, their injuries have healed. Like Malala, they moved to England to finish their schooling. Shazia Ramzan has a similar goal as Malala. "I'd like to complete my studies and go back home and help girls," she said.[4]

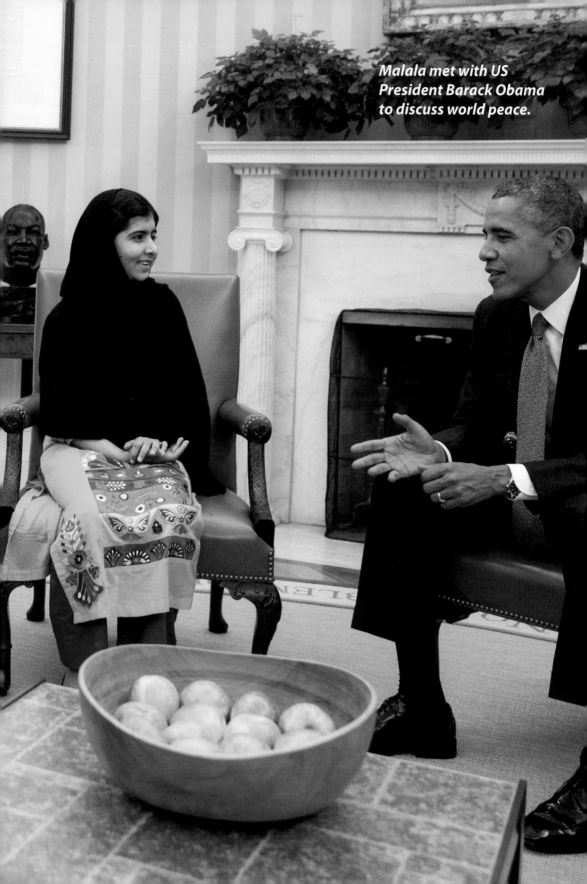

Malala met with US President Barack Obama to discuss world peace.

People around the world have been impressed by Malala's courage. The shooting could have caused her to back away from pursuing her goals. Instead, it reinforced her dedication in seeing that every child receives an education.

Since the shooting, Malala has received many awards for her work as an education activist. In October 2013, she received the European Union's prestigious Human Rights Award and the country of Nigeria created Malala Day in her honor.

On her sixteenth birthday, Malala spoke to the United Nations in New York City. She wore a white shawl that had belonged to her beloved Pakistani leader, Benazir Bhutto. Bhutto's family gave it to Malala as a token of their appreciation for her efforts to help the world's poor.

Wearing the shawl reminded Malala of Bhutto's bravery. Speaking to more than 400 world leaders, she said, "Thousands of people have been killed by terrorists and millions injured. I'm just one. I speak not for myself, but for those without voices, those who have fought for their rights. Their right to live in peace. Their right to be treated with dignity. Their right to be educated."[1]

She has personally met with many world leaders, including Queen Elizabeth of England and US President Barack Obama.

In 2014, Malala accepted the International Children's Peace Prize, which is voted on by children around the world. It is given to people who have achieved much in helping children worldwide. Malala, thrilled with the award, donated the $50,000 prize money to rebuilding schools in Gaza, a war-torn strip of land bordered by the Mediterranean Sea, Egypt, and Israel, and owned by Palestine.

Perhaps the most highly respected honor she received occurred in December 2014 in Oslo, Norway: the Nobel Peace Prize. Alfred Nobel was a wealthy inventor who left his life savings to a special fund that would award people who 'have conferred the greatest benefit on mankind.'[2] Since 1901, the Nobel Prizes have been presented annually on December 10, the anniversary of Nobel's death. The winners are called laureates.

Malala was the youngest recipient and the first Pakistani to be given the Nobel Peace Prize. She focused her acceptance speech in front of hundreds of people on the subject of education. "Why is

Malala's awards include the Sakharov Prize for Freedom of Thought from the European Parliament president Martin Schulz, in Strasbourg, France.

building tanks for war so easy but building schools so hard?" she asked.[3]

Malala shared the award with Kailash Satyarthi of India. Satyarthi, a Hindu, was given the award for his work against child labor. "This prize gives a message of love to people between Pakistan and India and between different religions," Malala said in her acceptance speech. "It does not matter the color of your skin, language you speak, religion you believe. We should respect each other. We should all fight for our rights, the rights of children and women and every human being."[4] Malala and Satyarthi agreed to divide equally the prize money of approximately $1.1 million for their causes.[5]

Malala has used her prize money to establish the Malala Fund (Malala.org). This group organizes educational resources for the 66 million children around the world who still do not have access to education.

Not everyone appreciates Malala's

In December 2014, Malala was honored to accept the Nobel Peace Prize in Oslo, Norway.

Malala Yousafzai

All I want is education, and I am afraid of no one.

For most of her life, Malala has worked for freedom for oppressed people around the world.

determination and efforts. Some people believe her work has been a scheme for her family to move to the England. Others think she speaks so often about the problems with military, education, and governments because she only wants attention.[6]

Malala doesn't listen to negative comments or doubts about her cause. "I had two choices," she tells people. "I could suffer terrorism and wait to be killed. Or I could speak up and be killed. I chose the second."[7]

For encouragement, Malala looks to US civil rights leader of the 1960s, Martin Luther King, Jr. "He had a dream that people of all colors would be treated equally," she said. "We've seen that dream come true."[8]

"Let us pick up our books and our pens," she wrote in her biography. "They are our most powerful weapons. One child, one teacher, one book, and one pen can change the world."[9]

Malala has shown the world just how powerful these tools can be.

1997   Malala is born on July 12, in Swat Valley, Mingora, Pakistan.

2007   Benazir Bhutto, Pakistan's former prime minister, is assassinated. The Taliban arrives in Swat Valley and begins bombing Pakistani schools. By the end of the following year, they have destroyed 400 schools.

2009   In January, the Taliban prohibits all girls from attending school. Malala agrees to write, in secret, a blog about life under Taliban rule for the BBC. In May, Malala's family and thousands of others leave Swat Valley because of the war. By August, the army drives out the Taliban, Malala's family returns home, and girls like Malala return to school.

2010   Malala regularly provides interviews with foreign news correspondents in Pakistan.

2011   Malala is awarded Pakistan's first National Peace Prize, which is later renamed the Malala Prize. She is nominated for the International Children's Peace Prize.

2012   The Taliban posts threats against Malala's life on the Internet. In October, Malala is shot by a terrorist and flown to a hospital in Birmingham, England. Her family flies there to be with her. Malala undergoes many surgeries and therapy to recover from her injuries.

2013   Malala's family moves to Birmingham. Malala enrolls in school there in April. She accepts the International Children's Peace Prize and speaks to the United Nations in New York City on her sixteenth birthday. She receives the European Union's Human Rights Award. She is nominated for the Nobel Peace Prize. She meets Queen Elizabeth of England and US President Barack Obama.

2014   The country of Nigeria creates Malala Day in her honor. Malala receives the International Children's Peace Prize. In December, she receives the Nobel Peace Prize in Oslo, Norway. She establishes the Malala Fund to help raise money for children's education worldwide.

2015   Malala's audio biography version wins Grammy Award for Best Children's Album. Malala Yousafzai welcomes Pakistan school massacre survivor and family to Birmingham.

Chapter 1. Nightmare

1. "Full Amanpour Malala Interview." CNN. Online video clip. Youtube, October 22, 2013. Web. December 12, 2014.

2. Malala Yousafzai and Christina Lamb, *I Am Malala: The Girl Who Stood Up for Education and Was Shot by the Taliban* (New York: Little, Brown and Co., 2013), p. 278.

3. Ibid., p. 129.

4. Ibid., p. 131.

5. Ibid., p. 144.

6. Ibid., p. 158.

7. Laura Smith-Spark, "Nobel Peace Prize," CNN. October 10, 2014. Web. December 11, 2014.

Chapter 2. Living Among the Taliban

1. Malala Yousafzai and Christina Lamb, *I Am Malala: The Girl Who Stood Up for Education and Was Shot by the Taliban* (New York: Little, Brown and Co., 2013), p. 142.

2. Ibid., p. 146.

3. Ibid., p. 137.

4. Ibid., p. 286.

5. "Full Amanpour Malala Interview." CNN. Online video clip. YouTube, October 22, 2013. Accessed December 12, 2014.

6. Ibid., p. 161.

7. Ibid., p. 89.

8. Ibid., p. 166.

9. Ibid., p. 141.

Chapter 3. Three Shots

1. Malala Yousafzai and Christina Lamb, *I Am Malala: The Girl Who Stood Up for Education and Was Shot by the Taliban* (New York: Little, Brown and Co., 2013), p. 312.

2. Ibid., p. 141.

3. Ibid., p. 225–7.

4. Ibid., p. 215.

Chapter 4. A New Life

1. Malala Yousafzai and Christina Lamb, *I Am Malala: The Girl Who Stood Up for Education and Was Shot by the Taliban* (New York: Little, Brown and Co., 2013), p. 290.

2. "Full Amanpour Malala Interview," CNN, Online video clip. YouTube, October 22, 2013. Accessed December 12, 2014.

3. "I Want to Become Prime Minister of Pakistan: Malala Yousafzai," *Times of India,* October 11, 2013. Accessed December 11, 2014.

4. "The Other Girls Shot in Taliban Attack on Malala," *The National,* October 9, 2013. Accessed December 1, 2014.

Chapter 5. Moving Forward

1. "Malala Yousafzai UN Speech: Girl Shot in Attack by Taliban Gives Address," *The New York Times,* July 12, 2013. Accessed December 13, 2014.

2. "Alfred Nobel's Will," The Official Site of the Nobel Prize, Accessed February 14, 2015, http://www.nobelprize.org/alfred_nobel/will/

3. "Malala Yousafzai Speech, Nobel Peace Prize Presentation Ceremony, Oslo." Online video clip. YouTube. *TV5 News,* December 10 2014. Accessed December 11, 2014.

4. Ibid.

5. Laura Smith-Spark, "Nobel Peace Prize," CNN. October 10, 2014. Web. December 11, 2014.

6. Mehreen Zahra-Malik, "Malala, Survivor of Taliban, Resented in Pakistan Hometown," *The Star,* October 11, 2013. Accessed December 11, 2014.

7. Malala Yousafzai Nobel Prize Speech.

8. "Full Amanpour Malala Interview," CNN, Online video clip. YouTube, October 22, 2013. Accessed December 12, 2014.

9. Yousafzai, p. 310.

FURTHER READING

Books

Abouraya, Karen Leggett. *Malala Yousafzai: Warrior with Words.* Great Neck, NY: StarWalk Kids Media, 2014.

McCarney, Rosemary. *Dear Malala, We Stand with You.* New York: Crown Books for Young Readers, 2014.

Rowell, Rebecca. *Malala Yousafzai: Education Activist.* Minneapolis, MN: Abdo Publishing, 2014.

Winter, Jeanette. *Malala, a Brave Girl from Pakistan/Iqbal, a Brave Boy from Pakistan: Two Stories of Bravery.* New York: Beach Lane Books, 2014.

Yousafzai, Malala, with Christina Lamb. *I Am Malala: The Girl Who Stood Up for Education and Was Shot by the Taliban.* New York: Little, Brown and Co., 2013.

Yousafzai, Malala, and Patricia McCormick. *I Am Malala: How One Girl Stood Up for Education and Changed the World* (Young Readers Edition). New York: Little, Brown Books for Young Readers, 2014.

Works Consulted

Corder, Mike. "Malala Receives Children's Peace Prize." *Huffington Post,* September 6, 2013.

Cullinane, Susannah, and Brent Swails. "Malala to Boko Haram: Stop Misusing Islam." CNN, July 15, 2014.

"Full Amanpour Malala Interview." CNN. YouTube, October 22, 2013. Accessed December 12, 2014.

"I Want to Become Prime Minister of Pakistan: Malala Yousafzai." *Times of India*, October 11, 2013. Accessed December 11, 2014.

"Malala Wins World's Children's Prize 2014 in Sweden, Called the 'Children's Nobel.'" Associated Press Online, October 29, 2014. Accessed December 11, 2014.

"Malala Yousafzai to Obama's Face: Drones Fuel Terrorism." *The Young Turks*, October 14, 2013. Accessed December 11, 2014.

"Malala Yousafzai Speech, Nobel Peace Prize Presentation Ceremony, Oslo." *TV5 News*, December 10, 2014. Accessed December 11, 2014.

"Malala Yousafzai, the Teenager Who Was Shot by the Taliban, Meets Queen Elizabeth." *ABC News*. Online video clip. YouTube, October 18, 2013. Accessed December 11, 2014.

"Malala Yousafzai UN Speech: Girl Shot in Attack by Taliban Gives Address." *The New York Times*, July 12, 2013. Accessed December 13, 2014.

"Malala Yousafzai Wins EU's Sakharov Human Rights Prize." BBC, October 10, 2013. Accessed December 13, 2014.

"The Other Girls Shot in Taliban Attack on Malala." *The National*, October 9, 2013. Accessed December 1, 2014.

Smith-Spark, Laura. "Malala Yousafzai and Kailash Satyarthi Share Nobel Peace Prize." *CNN*, October 10, 2014. Accessed December 1, 2014.

Smith-Spark, Laura. "Nobel Peace Prize." *CNN*, October 10, 2014. Accessed December 11, 2014.

Zahra-Malik, Mehreen. "Malala, Survivor of Taliban, Resented in Pakistan Hometown." *The Star*, October 11, 2013. Accessed December 11, 2014.

On the Internet

Malala Fund

    Malala.org

Official Site of the Nobel Prize

    http://www.nobelprize.org

GLOSSARY

activist (AK-tih-vist)—Someone who works to change a political or moral wrong.

assassinate (uh-SAS-in-ayt)—To murder a well-known person.

burqa (BUR-kah)—A loose outer garment worn by women in some Islamic traditions to cover their bodies when in public.

cochlear implant (KOH-klee-ur IM-plant)—A surgically implanted electronic device that allows a deaf person to hear.

confidential (kon-fih-DENT-shul)—Strictly private.

democracy (duh-MAH-kruh-see)—A form of government in which the people hold supreme power (such as by the right to vote and to participate in government decisions).

dictatorship (dik-TAY-tor-ship)—A form of government in which one person holds absolute, often overbearing power or control.

endow (en-DOW)—To provide with a permanent fund or source of income.

exile (EK-zyl)—To be forbidden to live in or even visit one's native land.

haven (HAY-vun)—A place of shelter and safety.

Hindu (HIN-doo)—A person, especially of northern India, whose religion includes the belief in being reborn on earth and the idea of escaping earthly evils.

Internally Displaced Person (IDP)—Someone who is forced to flee his or her home but who remains within his or her country's borders.

Islam—The religious faith of Muslims.

Koran (kor-AN)—The sacred text of Islam accepted as the foundation of Islamic law, religion, culture, and politics.

laureate (LAW-ree-ut)—A person who has been given a great award.

martyr (MAR-tur)—Person who is put to death or endures great suffering on behalf of a belief, principle, or cause.

Muslim (MOOS-lim or MUZ-lim)—The religion, law, or civilization of Islam; also, a person whose religion is Islam.

Nobel (noh-BEL) **Peace Prize**—One of five prizes created by inventor Alfred Nobel, along with prizes in Chemistry, Physics, Physiology, and Literature, to honor those who have made the greatest contributions to mankind in their field.

omen (OH-men)—Anything believed to foretell a good or evil event.

prime minister—The chief of government.

Taliban (TAL-ih-ban)—An extremist Muslim group in Afghanistan that often uses violence to achieve its goals.

terrorist (TAYR-or-ist)—A person who frightens others in order to gain power.

United Nations—The international organization committed to maintaining international peace and security. Starting with 51 countries in 1945, its membership now includes 193 governments

Urdu (UR-doo)—One of the official languages of Pakistan.